ABOUT  ﹐HOR

Gunvor Johansson was born and grew up in the north of Sweden, where you will find spectacular displays of northern lights in the winter and in the summer the midnight sun. In her late teens she came to England and her first year was spent in Guildford as an au-pair. She studied English at Guildford collage and intended to stay only for a year. She is still here and now lives on the south coast, near Chichester.

Tula's Troll is the first in a series of books about a small troll, whose ancestors came across to Scotland, from Scandinavia, by hiding in the Vikings' long boats.

Also by Gunvor Johansson

The Water People's Secret
and the sequel
Alice and Friends in her Secret World.

The need to save the oceans from pollution and
destruction is reflected in these books.

To Eva

Happy Christmas 2016

TULA'S TROLL

Gunvor Johansson

Enjoy!

Gunvor Johansson

BRIARFIELD
PRESS

ISBN 978-1539649151

Book design by The Art of Communication
www.artofcomms.co.uk

Dedication

To Isabelle - great granddaughter - the light of my life.

Acknowledgements

My thanks to Hilary Deadman and Lorna Howarth
for their friendly help and support during the writing of this book.

To Pam Nockemann for her help with the editing.

Also my thanks to my friends at Fareham Writer's Group
for their helpful comments.

TULA'S TROLL

GUNVOR JOHANSSON

A sharp cry! A whimper! It comes from the undergrowth of the fir-tree branches. Tula stands as still as a statue. Tense and alert, she listens. Another cry and the branches move sharply up and down. Fallen red and yellow autumn leaves from the nearby oak are sent dancing into the air. She takes a deep breath, and catches the smell of the fresh pine trees. Is it a trapped animal, a wild boar? No, it must be smaller, she thinks. Perhaps, an injured hare?

The branches shake again much more

violently. Amongst the rustle, she can hear sobs. She steps forward and a twig snaps under her foot with a loud crack. At once everything is still. Like Tula, the forest holds its breath. For several minutes she waits, uncertain what to do. But then the rustle and shaking starts again.

She picks up a stick and with it parts the branches of the fir tree. Huge terrified eyes stare back at her from under bushy eyebrows. A piercing scream escapes her and she steps back. At this the creature covers his head with both arms and weeps uncontrollably, his tiny shoulders shudder. Her scream dies away. Whatever this is, it won't hurt me, she thinks. It's more frightened than I am.

'It's all right. It's all right,' she repeats and tries to steady her voice. 'I won't hurt you. Can I help?'

The wailing stops at once, but the shoulders still tremble. Slowly the creature lifts his head. Tear drops as big as pearls cling to his rosy cheeks and he wipes them away with the back of his hairy hand.

Tula stares at his large ears and inhales sharply. 'You're a troll!' she gasps, her heart gallops. 'My goodness! A troll here in Scotland!'

'Yes, and you're a human. Go away! Leave me alone!'

'Why?' She moves closer.

'No!' shrieks the troll and shrinks back. 'Don't touch me!'

'But I want to help. You're stuck, I can see that. You'll never be able to free yourself.'

'I will! I will!' The troll pulls hard on his left leg, which remains firmly jammed under a tree root.

'See! You can't do it. Let me!' Tula leans over and the troll begins to holler at the top of his voice. 'OK. I won't touch you. But I'll sit down here on the moss and wait. If you can't free yourself soon you'll let me help, won't you?'

The troll grabs hold of his leg and yanks it. His face turns purple with the effort and his big lips are pinched together. No good. He covers his eyes and cries so hard his whole body rocks.

'Oh dear.' Tula leans over to stroke the back of his head; his jet black hair is coarse to touch. Her nose twitches as she catches a whiff of unwashed troll.

The troll sits bolt upright. His black eyes are wide with horror, 'You touched me!' he yells. 'Oh no! Oh no!'

'Why can't I touch you?'

'You don't understand,' the troll whimpers. 'Not supposed to show myself to humans. Never mind talking to you. You only see us in Fairy Tales.'

'Yes, that's how I know what you are. I've seen pictures of you.'

The troll looks searchingly at Tula, 'You're not big, perhaps you're not human?' he asks hopefully.

'I'm afraid, I am. I'm a child human. My name is Tula. What's yours?'

'Huva is my name. Now go away. Leave me alone!'

'Why won't you let me help you?' Tula asks softly.

'You don't understand. If I let you save my life, I'll have to be your obedient servant.'

'But I'm not saving your life. I'll only help to free you.'

'Not true! No one will come to look for me, so I'll die here. I've been banished from my land.'

'What do you mean? Banished.'

'The Troll Court has taken away my key, so I can't unlock the door to Troll Land. They say I'm not a proper troll. I should be bad and scary, but I can't.' A deep sigh escapes the troll. He looks at Tula, 'But I did scare you, didn't I? You screamed.'

'Yes, but that was before I got a good look at you.'

'See, I can't be a bad troll. I cry all the time.'

'Well, let me free you anyway.'

'No, I'd rather die than be saved by a human and I don't want to become your servant.'

Huva picks up a leaf and wipes his eyes.

'Look, I don't want a servant. I don't need one,' Tula smiles.

'I'd have to. It's the law of my land,' Huva snivels.

'But nobody needs to know. I won't tell anyone.'

'I would, if I get back home! Trolls can't keep a secret,' his voice quivers.

'Well, just make sure you do,' Tula answers a little impatient.

'It's no good I can't help myself.'

'This is silly! How long would you have to be my servant?'

'Forever.' Huva hangs his head, 'unless...'

'Unless what?'

'Unless I save your life, we'll be quits then.' Huva squints up at Tula.

'Hmm, that could be tricky,' she frowns.

'See! Go away and let me die.' Huva cries out and big tear drops run down his cheeks.

'I will not!' Tula shouts and springs forward, and tugs at the tree root above his foot with all her might.

All the while Huva hollers at the top of his voice, 'No-o-o, no-o, no-o!'

Tula hears a pop as the root gives way and she falls backwards into the fir-tree branches. She picks herself up and crawls out on all fours. The ribbon, which holds her dark hair in place, has come undone and she ties it back into a ponytail. Huva is sitting on a tuft of grass; he rubs his foot and glares at her.

'Why haven't you run away?' Tula gets up and brushes wet leaves from her jeans.

'I can't. I've to stay with you now.'

'Don't be ridiculous! You can go.'

'Your fault, you shouldn't have saved me.' Huva picks up another leaf but this time he blows his nose with it. The tears leave streaks on his muddy face and his huge sorrowful eyes stare back at her.

'Oh no, I think you mean it,' she cries out in alarm and sits down next to him. 'I can't take a troll home with me,' she says pleading. 'You must understand that. Besides you smell.'

'I have to go with you,' Huva insists.

'Look, let me explain why you can't.'

'All right, but it won't make any difference.' Huva stops crying.

'I'm ten years old. I live with my mum and dad in the cottage at the edge of the forest. It's not far, just down the path over there. My dad is the forest ranger. I go to school where I learn lots of things. I go every day and you can't possibly come with me. In any case what are you doing in Scotland? I thought trolls lived only in Scandinavia.'

'Some of us came over in the Vikings' longboats. We become shadows, unless you look for us, you can't see us. We move about in your world, but we avoid humans.'

'You do! Like shadows! That's scary.' Tula's eyes flash wide. 'How old are you?' she asks, calmer now.

'I don't know, I could be centuries old.'

'You don't look old. Is it true that you stay bad and naughty all your life?'

'Yes, but I'm not bad and naughty. That's my problem.' Huva jumps as a loud buzz comes from Tula's pocket.

'It's OK. No need to be scared, it's my

mobile. It's a text from Mum.' Tula taps in a reply to her mother and slips the phone back into her pocket.

All the while Huva remains silent.

'You should go home now. I must, I have homework to do. I came to pick pine-cones to take to school. But I'd like to meet you tomorrow afternoon. Can we?'

Huva stands up and she sees how small he is; his head only reaches to her waist. He tucks his hands into the pockets of his red shorts, his upper body is bare and hairy and so are his feet. He nods at her as she leaves. After a short distance she turns around to wave. Huva is right behind her. 'Go home!' Her voice is firm and she carries on walking. But she stops when she hears a rustle of leaves.

'Stop following me! Go home!' she shouts and stamps the ground. Huva stands rock still, and stares back at her with a blank expression on his face. He begins to fade, soon he is only a shadow, which disappears amongst the fir trees.

Tula stands gawking, her mouth wide open,

'Oh, it was scary to see him vanish like that. But he's gone, at last. Thank goodness!' She continues her walk home. She does not notice the shadow, which follows her from tree to tree.

'Tula, have you got your pine-cones?' Her mother asks as she closes the oven door.

'No, Mum.'

'You'll need them for the project tomorrow. What will you be doing with them?'

'We'll spray them with gold and silver paint to make decorations. But I forgot and didn't pick any.'

'You forgot! How come?'

'I met a troll, Mum.'

'Well, that would be a good excuse, if they

existed, but we know they don't,' her mother laughs.

'That's what I thought,' Tula answers.

'I feel a draught. You must've left the front door open.'

'Sorry, Mum, I thought I closed it.' She runs back into the hall and gives the door a push. As she returns to the kitchen, a shadow vanishes up the stairs.

'Help me lay the table.' Her mother hands her knives and forks, 'It's your last day before half-term. Made any plans? You'll have a whole week off.'

'I'll think of something, Mum.' Tula looks up as the door opens and her father fills the frame. He is tall and strong with unruly brown hair and blue eyes, which are never serious. He puts an arm around her mother's waist and hugs her.

'What's in the oven, Kate? It smells delicious.'

'It's an apple pie.' Tula's mother laughs and pushes her husband away.

'Mum, I'm going to my room. Please, call me when dinner is ready.'

In her room Tula catches a whiff of a bad

smell. Odd, she thinks. She sniffs the air and opens a window. She picks up her hair brush, and stands in front of the full length mirror. Her dark fringe almost covers her eyebrows and she sweeps it away to reveal cornflower blue eyes.

Suddenly the troll's reflection appears in the mirror. She screams and drops the brush. At her scream Huva covers his ears and his lips tremble.

'Oh, it's you. Why are you here? Go away!' she hisses. Her father's footsteps are racing up the stairs. Huva's ears prick up and he begins to fade. By the time her father bursts into the room Huva has turned into a barely detectable shadow. He disappears behind a chair.

'It's OK, Dad. Sorry, I screamed. It was a spider, I threw it out.' She points to the open window.

'But you're not afraid of spiders!' her father looks astonished.

'It was huge. Enormous!' Tula crosses her fingers behind her back.

As soon as her father leaves the room, Huva

steps out of his shadow. His eyes are downcast and his body trembles.

'You scare easily considering you're a troll,' Tula frowns.

'Don't like shouting and I'm supposed to scare you.' His voice can barely be heard.

'But you did scare me.'

Huva's eyes light up, 'I did?'

'A little; jumping out like that.' Tula shrugs her shoulders, 'So it was you I smelt when I came in, but you'll have to leave now.'

'I can't. I'll stay. I'll be your shadow,' he squeaks.

'Don't be silly!'

'I mean it. I have to, because you saved me.' Huva straightens his shoulders and stands tall, he stares back at her.

'So you'll come with me to school every day, and sleep in my room at night? No way! I tell you. It won't happen.'

'It's too hot in here. I'll sleep outside under a tree.'

'Good!'

'But I'll always be behind you, as your

shadow, wherever you go.'

'How exactly does this shadowy thingy work?' Tula taps her bedside table with the brush, her mouth set in a tight line.

'My shadow will cling to you, but too faint for anyone to see.'

'Cling to me! Oh no! I don't like the sound of that. And they will smell you! My friends will think I've fallen into a dung heap.'

Now it is Huva's turn to shrug his shoulders. Tula pulls her eyebrows together deep in thought. After a minute she looks up, 'Is there really no other way to get rid of you?'

Huva shakes his head.

'OK. Listen! I'll have to find a few pine-cones before I go to school. You can scrub yourself in the forest lake. I'll put the shampoo and bath-gel in my satchel right now.'

'Wash in water!' he shouts, his eyes bulge.

Tula covers his mouth with her hand, 'Hush! My parents will hear you.'

'Trolls never wash. I won't do it! It might kill me.' Huva whispers, the colour drains away from his rosy face.

'It won't kill you, believe me. As my servant you'll have to do what I ask. That means a bath tomorrow. If you don't like it leave at once and never come back. No bath for you and no troll for me. So make up your mind, I'm busy.' Tula's eyes are boring right into him.

Huva's face goes blank and he disappears in front of her. A shadow moves over the floor; the door opens and shuts. Tula runs out onto the landing in time to see the front door close quietly.

Good! That scared him off, she thinks. I knew the bath would do the trick. I won't see him again. Good riddance! Although…, he was kind of cute. But I ask you, who'd want a troll around? They stink!

'Tula, off to school already?' her mother asks the next morning.

'Yes, Mum, I need to take ten pine-cones and I have to find them first.'

'But you haven't had breakfast.'

'It's OK. I've packed an extra apple and banana. I'll eat them on the way.'

'Make sure you do.' Her mother blows her a kiss.

As Tula walks past the birch tree in the back garden, she knows that the troll is behind her.

She can smell him. 'Not you again, I thought you'd gone,' she moans.

'Why? You know I can't.' Huva steps out of his shadow and becomes a troll, skipping along beside her. He picks up a stone and throws it with force, it hits a tree trunk. As it bounces back it strikes Tula's leg.

'Ouch! You did that on purpose!'

'As if I could.' A smile is playing on his lips. 'Think I enjoy being here? Don't like me, do you?'

'It's not that I don't like you. It's hard to explain. You're not supposed to exist. When I told Mum about you she didn't believe me. And don't think I've changed my mind, about the bath. I've still got the bath-gel in my satchel.'

Huva stops skipping and slows down to a halt, 'I'm not going this way. It leads to the lake.'

'Exactly! That's where we're going,' Tula smiles.

'Not coming. I won't wash!'

'If you insist on being my shadow, then I insist that you have a wash.'

Huva shudders and clutches the tops of his arms, close to tears. Tula watches him and her eyes soften, 'Sorry! I am really, I'll help you. You'd never do it well enough anyway.'

Further along, the path curves to the left and they stand in front of a small lake, which is surrounded on all sides by pine trees. The clear water has a tinge of green and sparkles in the early morning sunshine. Tula stretches out her arms in front of her, 'I call this the "hidden loch." Isn't it beautiful?'

Huva does not answer but drags his legs all the way to the water's edge, 'Don't make me,' he whimpers. 'I can't swim. I'm scared.' He digs his big toes into the soft earth; the water is lapping his feet.

Tula takes off her shoes and socks and pulls Huva into the water, 'It's not deep here. See, it's only reaching your knees. I'll hold onto you.' She pours the lavender gel on top of his shoulders.

'It's freezing,' he cries out.'

'Come on! Here is a flannel. Now wash. Properly!'

Huva's trembling increases and he sobs throughout the bath, 'I'm all wet. I've never been wet before.'

'Don't be such a cry baby. But you did well. Now I'll wash your hair.' Tula gets out the shampoo.

Huva clamps both hands down on top of his head, 'NO!' He leaps towards the shore but Tula bars his way. He stands trembling, his eyes are pleading, 'Not my hair, not my hair,' he moans.

But Tula vigorously rubs in the shampoo; the lather flies into the lake, and dots the water like cotton-wool balls. She rinses off, using a mug from her satchel and then sniffs his hair. 'That'll do, for now.

Another wash wouldn't hurt though.'

Huva is paralysed with fear; he stares in front of him with unblinking eyes. The water is dripping off him, his shorts cling to his hairy legs.

'All done. Come on now.' Tula steps out of the water, but Huva has not moved. 'Oh dear, you really are petrified. Here take my hand!' She leads him on to land and rubs him dry with her towel. Slowly he comes to life and inhales deeply. A huge grin spreads across his face. The colour returns to his cheeks. He runs his nose along the length of his arm and grins again.

'Well, I never! You actually like your new smell,' Tula beams.

'I do, I can't tell a lie. Must I have a bath to get it? Huva raises his huge black eyes to her.

'Afraid so. But it's time to go to school and you're not coming with me!'

'But I must,' Huva stares back at her.

Tula can hear the determination in his voice, 'Yes, I suppose you must, but it'll be a disaster,' she answers with a deep sigh. 'How is this day going to end?'

GUNVOR JOHANSSON

On the way to school Huva traipses along beside Tula. When they reach the edge of the forest he fades into a shadow on her back. Tula sneezes once, when she smells lavender and a second time when she smells troll. 'Thank goodness your shadow doesn't weigh anything. But you could do with another wash,' she says. A low moan comes from behind her.

'When we arrive at school, you will stay outside.'

'Want to come in.'

'But I don't want you to and you're supposed to be obedient,' Tula snaps. Huva murmurs in reply but she cannot make out what he is saying.

'Get off my back now.' Tula hisses as they enter the play-ground, 'You can spend the day here, better still go home.'

'I want to see school,' a whisper.

'You can't. Now get off!' Tula shakes herself and feels a pinch as his shadow leaves her.

Two of her best friends, Sue and Isla, run up to meet her and they chat away as they walk into the classroom and find their desks.

'What are you doing half-term?' Sue leans over to Tula.

Tula has no time to answer, because the teacher raps her ruler, 'Quiet! I want to tell you about...' she stops as the door opens and she waits, expectantly, but nobody comes in. 'Somebody hasn't closed this door properly.' The teacher walks over and pulls it shut.

Tula's eyes open wide, between the desks a small shadow makes its way towards her. Because she has learnt to look for it, only she is able to spot it. Soon she feels Huva's shadow jiggle about on her back. She wriggles her shoulders to make him fall off, but he clings on, 'Oh no,' she moans.

'Are you all right?' Sue asks.

Tula nods, 'Yes, just a bit of an itch,' she stammers. She shakes herself again, more vigorously this time, as Huva is twitching restlessly.

'Are you sure you're OK?' Sue gives her an odd look.

Isla, who sits at the desk in front, turns around and raises her eyebrows, 'What's that smell?'

I must get rid of him, Tula thinks, my friends can smell him. 'Get lost!' her whisper is low, but Isla hears her.

'Me?' Isla says with an astonished look on her face.

'No, not you.'

'Who then?'

'Forget it, I was just thinking out loud,' Tula tries to explain.

'You were thinking it! That doesn't make it any better.'

'Isla! Nothing to do with you, believe me.

We're friends.'

'OK.' Isla turns away with a puzzled expression on her face.

As Huva slips off her back, he gives her arm a hard nip. His shadow moves along the row of desks. She bites her teeth together, to stop herself from calling out.

'Something smells,' says Rory, who sits near to where Huva is standing. 'Aaghh! Stop pinching me that hurts!' Rory cries out and elbows Sam, who is next to him.

'I didn't,' Sam stares.

'You did so!'

'Och, I did not!' Sam bangs his hand down on the desk. I know who did, Tula thinks.

The teacher's voice booms, 'Quiet! Order!'

'I'm moving desk.' Rory takes a few steps but trips up, luckily he does not fall over.

'Rory, go back to your desk and sit down.' The teacher's firm voice calls out.

Rory does as he is told, but he glares at Sam and hisses, 'You tripped me up,' as he takes his seat.

Huva has got it in for him, Tula thinks, perhaps

he has learnt to be a naughty troll after all. But I wish he wouldn't pinch every time he's upset.

Huva's shadow moves up to the window, which quietly opens. Tula sees him climb onto the sill, where his shadow gives the pane a darker shade. He leans out and falls away. As this happens there is a flicker of light and some pupils turn their heads towards the window. There is nothing to be seen.

'I'm freezing. Who opened the window?' a girl whines, and pulls her cardigan across her chest. She hugs her arms and looks accusingly at the boy next to her.

'I didn't. It opened by itself,' he protests.

'I'll close it!' Tula jumps up and rushes over to the window. Huva's shadow is outside and she knows he is all right. Thank goodness we're on the ground floor, she thinks.

'Thank you, Tula.' The teacher raps her ruler on the desk, harder this time, 'After half-term I want you to write an historical essay. It shouldn't be more than 500 words long. I'm letting you know now, as some of you might like to prepare for it during the holidays.'

'I won't,' says a boy, who sits two rows in front of Tula. The teacher ignores him.

'I'm going to Tenerife with my parents,' a girl says.

'It's all right. I didn't say that you had to. Only that some of you might,' the teacher explains. 'To get ideas you can look it up on-line, or you'll find history books in the library.'

When Tula leaves the playground after school, and takes the forest path home, Huva's shadow joins her. Tula is tight-lipped and ignores him.

'Talk to me!'

'I don't want to,' Tula snaps.

'You're angry.'

'Yes, you're a disaster. I can't have you hanging around. You nearly started a war in my class. Go home!'

'I want to but I can't, not without the key.' Huva leaves the shadow and walks beside her.

'Where is it?'

'You wouldn't understand.'

'Try me!'

'I'll have to climb down the Century Ladder.

The key can only be found in the year of 1545. Don't want to go; it's very, very dangerous.' Huva kicks a stone with his bare foot, 'Ohoo, aaghh.' He cries out and jumps about on one leg, holding his foot with both hands.

'Stop wailing! Now you know what it feels like when you pinch. It hurts. Serves you right.'

Huva grimaces as he sits down on the path and rubs his big toe, 'The Troll Court says that going down the Century Ladder will make me a scary and proper troll.'

'Sounds weird.'

'I knew, you wouldn't understand.'

'OK. Let's start again. What's the Century Ladder?'

'It's a ladder, which will take me back in time.'

'Can you really do that?' Tula's eyes are wide open in astonishment.

'Yes, wish I had kept my mouth shut. It's too risky.'

'I know you can't tell a lie. I'll come with you.'

'Would you really do that for me?' Huva's eyes begin to shine.

'It will be one step nearer to getting rid of you.'

'Oh,' Huva's smile changes into a frown and he stares at the ground. 'I won't go. Even if I find the key, I can't go home.' Huva is close to tears, 'Not until I've saved your life.'

'I agree. It's not likely to happen, but one thing at a time. It will be a start to get the key. As my servant, you'll have to do as I ask.'

Huva's shoulders are crunched, 'Yes,' he answers in a low whisper.

'But where will we have to go?'

'The key is hidden in Southsea Castle, that's down south in a town called Portsmouth. The ladder will take us to the right place.'

'I've heard of Portsmouth. It will be exciting. Where do we find that ladder?'

'We go to the Leaning Stone in the forest. It's magical.' A big smile spreads across his face, 'I live there.'

'I've seen it, I went with my dad. He says the stone was carried there by ice during the Ice Age. It's defying gravity. The way it leans over the ravine, it should fall down. No one can explain why it doesn't.'

Huva laughs so much, he has to hold onto his round tummy, 'We did it! It won't fall down as long as our troll magic holds it up.'

'Amazing!' Tula's eyes are the size of saucers. 'We'll go tomorrow!' Huva's laugh is catching and it makes Tula laugh as well.

'Clothes you wear aren't right.' Huva snorts between laughs.

'I know that. Mum has got a book about historical clothes with pictures. I'll look at it when I get in.'

As they reach the garden gate Huva says, 'Don't like your school.'

'Good. Perhaps you won't come with me again?'

'Have to. I asked you not to save me, but you wouldn't listen!' Huva glares at her and the merriment has gone out of his voice.

'I though I was helping you. I couldn't leave you there.'

'Big mistake!' Huva's voice is miserable and he shakes his head. 'I'll wait for you in the morning. I'll sleep under the pine tree.' He fades away. Tula shrugs her shoulders and skips into the house, glad to be rid of her shadow. If only for now.

The next morning Tula puts on a pair of baggy track suit bottoms, which she tucks into knee-length white socks. She selects a brown t-shirt with long sleeves and on top a short brown cape, which her granny gave her for Christmas last year.

'Why are you dressed up like that, Tula? You look more like a boy today,' her mother says.

'I'm going into the forest, Mum. I don't want to spoil my jeans.'

Her mother raises her eyebrows, 'Really? Well, don't go far. Hope you'll find lots of pine-cones.'

Tula nods and leaves the house, but she does not tell her mother the real reason for going out. She makes her way to where Huva is waiting.

'I dressed to pretend I'm a boy and Mum said I look like one. And I've brought this for you. It's too small for me.' From inside her cape Tula pulls out a yellow waist-coat and holds it out to Huva.

'For me!' Huva's eyes shine and he blushes. He gingerly takes the waist-coat and puts it on. He leaves the large yellow buttons undone and his hairy chest is still showing.

'That's better; you're more properly dressed now.' Tula nods.

Huva smiles broadly, and strokes his new coat with both hands, 'But you're too clean and ...' He sniffs the air, 'You smell sweet! Come with me!' Huva leads the way to where a patch of ground is particularly muddy, 'Roll in it!'

'Are you mad?' she cries. 'No way!'

'Then I'll fix it!' Huva shouts and jumps into the puddle; the mud flies up into the air and splashes her all over.

'You're crazy.' But Tula laughs, the mud drips off Huva's hair too and a smile lurks at the corner of his mouth. 'You're getting naughtier. Will I do now?' Her clothes are splattered; her socks and black trousers are covered in brown specks. Huva is pleased with the result and they set off through the forest.

After twenty minutes they arrive at the Leaning Stone. She remembers her dad saying that it is six metres long and five metres high. It is almost square. It could have been cut with a huge knife. The shape is that of a slightly askew box. It is covered by green and grey moss.

'Talk to him, or he won't let you in.' Huva says.

'Talk to the stone...' Tula stops, 'you're making fun of me.'

'No, you know I can't tell lies.' Huva's face is serious.

'OK. What do I say to it?'

'He! Not it.' Huva says.

'Sorry! Can I call him Mr Stone?'

'His name is Sten. I'll wake him up. He's

asleep.'

'He is?' Tula stares at the stone.

Huva puts his hand on a yellow mossy patch and pats it gently. There is a grating noise, followed by a rumble. Two large patches of moss

flip up, to show grey stony eyes. Underneath, another patch splits open to reveal a mouth.

Tula holds her breath.

'Yes?' The voice is dark and gravelly. 'Oh, it's you, Huva. Where have you been all this time?'

'With this girl, Tula. We want to come in.'

'Would you now? But you can't get into Troll Land without your key.'

'I know. She'll help me to get it back. We're

going down the Century Ladder.'

'But she's a human child, Huva. How come?'

So Huva tells Sten the story about how he came to be Tula's servant.

'Have you told her that you both face grave danger down there?'

'Yes, but she's very stubborn.' Huva sneaks a sideways glance at Tula.

'I see.' Sten rumbles loudly and falls silent.

Tula stands still and looks down at the ground. This stone scares her. She is no longer sure about being here. After what seems a long moment, Sten turns his eyes on her and scrutinizes her. 'Does she speak?'

A shiver goes down her spine but she makes her voice strong, 'Good morning, Sten. Would you be so kind and let me come in,' she takes a deep breath, 'please, Sir.'

'She's polite enough,' Sten turns his gaze to Huva. 'All right, but she's your responsibility.' The eyes close up and a rumble can be heard from inside the stone. It grows louder and louder, whilst what was the mouth gets bigger and bigger. It becomes an opening large enough for Huva and Tula to enter.

Once they are inside the rumble starts again and the opening behind them closes. The chamber is in semi - darkness and her eyes take time to adjust. Huva is by her side. He whistles and glow-worms appear to show them the way.

'Light worms!' Tula exclaims, as one settles on her outstretched hand. She barely dares to breathe, in case it flies away. But it does anyway.

They are in a large empty room with a stone floor. There are five closed doors along the sides of the four walls. All have a name on them. The doors are too far away to read what it says, except for two. On the nearest one it is written: Troll Land in green letters, on the other it says: Witches' Land, in mauve colour. That door creaks open and eyes like coal stare at her. The face disappears and a black cat slinks out.

'It's Emily, she's my friend. One minute she's a witch, the next a cat.'

'What's behind the doors?' Tula whispers, afraid to raise her voice, and moves away from Emily.

'Different places.' Huva points, 'I live behind

the one with green letters. But now we'll find the Century Ladder and climb down. We'll get off it in 1545.'

'I remember from school that's the Tudor age. This is exciting; it will help me with my essay.'

'Urug is in charge of the Ladder. He will tell us how many steps to take, so we don't go to the wrong place.'

Tula touches her forehead, which has gone clammy, 'I'm not sure anymore. How is this possible?' she stammers.

'Have you changed your mind?' Huva asks hopefully. But Tula shakes her head and he leads her to a door on which is painted in gold letters: The Century Ladder.

GUNVOR JOHANSSON

Huva turns the knob, but the door will not open. He leans on it, and pushes with his shoulders. Nothing happens. 'Is it locked?' Tula asks.

'No, but he doesn't want us to go in,' Huva does not meet her eyes. 'Quite right too,' he mumbles.

'Who is he? And why?'

'Urug wants to stop us. It is dangerous to go back in time. Some people never come back. The Troll Court is punishing me by sending me there. Sure you want to go?'

'Well, we've come this far...,' Tula drags her words. But quickly carries on with a firm voice, 'We need to get that key. I'll help you push.'

The door opens slowly and Tula steps over the threshold, Huva follows behind her. The room is dark. By the eerie glow from the light-worms, she can make out a round railing in the far corner. There are posters on the walls, with coloured frames, which make them stand out against the granite walls. The moment she passes by; each one illuminates in a different colour. One poster has got the heading Sixteenth Century and the frame lights up with an orange glimmer, when she stops in front of it. Tula squints at the notice and reads out loud, ARE YOU ABSOLUTELY SURE THAT YOU WANT TO GO DOWN THE CENTURY LADDER? IF SO READ ON... the text stops.

'But there's nothing more to read,' she cries out.

'You must answer,' Huva says.

'I am sure,' Tula's voice is firm.

Text appears: VERY WELL, CLIMB DOWN THE LADDER IN THE CORNER. YOU MUST START

EVERY STEP WITH YOUR RIGHT FOOT, REMEMBER YOUR RIGHT FOOT, AND A RUNG WILL BE VISIBLE. YOU MUST ALWAYS KEEP ONE HAND ON THE RAIL. ON NO ACCOUNT FORGET THAT. DO YOU UNDERSTAND?

Tula nods.

'Answer!' Huva pulls her arm.

'I do understand,' she blurts out.

WHICH YEAR DO YOU WANT? AND WHERE DO YOU WANT TO BE, WHEN YOU ARRIVE?

'The year of 1545; near Southsea Castle.' Tula replies and then quickly adds, 'in July, please, it's warmer then.'

ALL THE TIME YOUR MIND MUST CONCENTRATE ON YOUR DESTINATION. IF YOU DON'T YOU MAY NOT ARRIVE CLOSE TO IT. TAKE 545 STEPS DOWN AND YOU WILL BE THERE. LET GO OF THE HANDRAIL, BUT NOT BEFORE. REMEMBER 545. The notice goes blank.

Tula walks across the room to the railing in front of a circular hole. She peers down and shivers, 'Hmm, hmm.' She starts to speak but first clears her throat, 'There's nothing there, no steps...nothing,' she stops. 'Only a handrail, which disappears ...,' she stops again. 'Into a black hole!' she cries out. 'I'm not sure,' her voice quivers.

'I know. Scary, isn't it? Shall we go home?' Huva whinges and pulls her towards the door, his eyes are full of fear.

Tula hesitates for several moments, 'No, let's do it! We will find the key. I don't want you around for ever. I'll go first.'

'Why don't you like me?'

'I do!' Tula whirls around to face him, 'Why did I say that? You're right, I don't.'

'I don't want to be with you either. But you made me. I want to go home to Troll Land.'

'Good! But we'll have to go down here first. Come on then!'

With a tight grip on the handrail she lowers her shaking right foot into the hole and a rung appears beneath her. As she climbs backwards, she carefully checks that each rung will take her weight, by pressing down hard on it. 'One,' she counts, 'two, three.' The glow-worms have attached themselves to the walls and Huva is directly above her. 'I'll count out loud. Don't interrupt me, or I might forget how far we've got. In case I do, try to remember the last number. This is terribly important.' Huva mumbles in agreement.

Many minutes go by, '303, 304.'

Huva is panting, 'I'm tired. Legs ache,' he mutters under his breath.

'OK. We'll have a rest. I forget that your legs are shorter than mine. But remember 304.' Tula examines the surroundings but cannot see much in the darkness. The glow-worms only show up a grey background and the air is cold. Tula reaches out to touch the stone wall, and she can smell the damp. She shivers and wipes the mould off her fingers. After only a minute or two she says, 'Let's carry on, Huva.'

Some time later Tula announces, '545, we've arrived! Just as well, as my legs are wobbly.' Huva clings on with one hand; and rubs his feet with the other.

'Step down next to me. We should hold hands when we let go of the railing, to be sure we arrive in the same place. I wonder where? Do you know, Huva?'

In the dim light Tula can see Huva's face turn green, his eyes wide and he answers with a whimper, 'No!'

'Are you afraid?' Tula asks. 'I'm not.'

'You should be, Tula. You should be very afraid!' Huva's thin voice can barely be heard.

'Be brave! Here's my hand. On the count of three we'll let go. One, two, three-.'

Tula gasps as the wall in front of them dissolves and she is forced to close her eyes as a bright light fills the space. Strong winds grip hold of them. It is difficult to hold on to Huva's hand, as they are hurtled away at speed. The whirling air hits her face and takes her breath away. By the time the movement slows down she is gasping, and she inhales deeply. Huva is by her side and his eyes are tightly shut. The wind has changed into a white fluffy mist, on which they float downwards. With her free hand she touches the cloud, but there is nothing to feel.

She relaxes her grip on Huva's hand and he lets go. 'Oh no!' she cries. Huva sinks through the whiteness and disappears below her out of view.

A moment later she lands with a thump; causing a small cloud of rising dust. She stifles a sneeze, and sits very still for several moments. I'm in a haystack, in a barn, she thinks. This isn't Southsea Castle.

Old fashioned farm tools, straight from the pages of her history book, lean against the walls. A dank and musty smell fills the barn, and she pinches her nose. To turn sideways she puts her hand on the mud floor, 'It's poo!' she mutters. Amongst the straw are cow pats and rat droppings. With a grimace, she wipes her hand on the hay.

Thoughts spin around; is anyone else here? Why did Huva let go? He could be miles away! Her chest is tight and her breath short. I have done something really stupid. I might have to stay here for ever. I don't know how to get home. Her eyes fill up with tears. She wants to take a deep breath but the foul air stops her. With her head in her hands she rocks to and fro.

Suddenly there is a rustle and a rat the size of a small cat runs out in front of her, another one follows. They are unafraid and a short distance away they turn around to face her. Paralysed with fear Tula does not cry out. Jeeps! If there's one thing I'm scared of; that's it, she thinks. Without taking her eyes off the rats she crawls forwards, and reaches out to the tools in front of her. She picks up a rake and at her movement the

rats scurry away. Now there is another rustle in the hay, much stronger this time.

Tula stiffens, 'More rats! Lots of them! I can't stay here, they'll eat me alive.'

The noise from the back of the haystack gets louder. Tula stands up and moves forward, she raises the rake above her head; ready to strike it down. As she turns the corner of the haystack, she drops it, 'Huva!' she cries. He is sitting on the floor covered in straw with a deep frown on his face. Tula falls down on her knees and hugs him, 'Oh thank goodness you're here!' She laughs, with tears running down her cheeks. Huva's frown changes to a smile and his cheeks turn pink. He dusts off his short and hairy legs, and bends down to remove straw caught between his toes.

'Oh Huva! We really are in the sixteenth century. But how do we go home again? I never gave it a thought.'

'We need a ladder! Like that one!' Straw drops off his hair as he points at a ladder, which leads up to the loft of the barn. 'We climb up and we'll be whisked back.'

'Really? You mean that any ladder will do?'

Huva nods, 'Yeah, once we reach the top, it will take us to the Century Ladder.'

'There are rats here, I'm scared. Come on, let's leave.'

'I'll be your shadow and whisper in your ear. I can't be a troll here. If I show myself, we'll be burned at the stakes as witches.'

'What!' Tula's face turns white and her legs wobble, 'Oh jeeps, we can't let that happen.' She takes a step towards the ladder.

'Going home?' A big grin spreads across Huva's face.

The colour returns to Tula's cheeks, and she looks into Huva's eyes, 'No, certainly not.'

The barn door squeaks as she slowly opens it and it makes her jump. She listens for a few moments before she pushes the door open a few centimetres more. With a finger in front of her mouth, she signs to Huva to be quiet, and peers out.

GUNVOR JOHANSSON

It is day time and Tula can see three houses about ten metres away, but no people. She hears a booming noise; she knows it is not thunder. What could be making that noise? She slinks out and staying close to the wall, she makes her way to the back. In front of her is a dried up track, it leads to a road some distance away. A cart drawn by an ox passes by, followed by two men on horses. Tula presses up against the wall, but nobody looks in her direction. It is strange here, she thinks. The smell is different.

The air is fresher so I can smell the grass. Nothing is as I know it. She looks up at the sun and sighs, 'At least, you're the same.'

Still leaning against the barn wall she takes a deep breath, 'I must not be afraid, I must not be afraid,' she repeats over and over.

Now she can sense Huva's shadow on her back and in her right ear he quivers, 'That makes two of us.'

'What do we do now?'

'Let's go to where the noise is. Must be Portsmouth.' Huva says reluctantly.

'If not we're in the wrong place, but I'm scared to meet the people.' Tula looks down at her clothes.

'You're dirty enough to fit in now. But we can go home.'

'It's tempting, Huva. But we must get the key back.'

Tula steps onto the dusty track in front of them and walks along in the furrows made by the deep ruts. Soon they reach the road. To each side are fields, some of them with sheep, others with cattle. Houses, all with roofs of straw, are situated away from the road, but there is no sign of life. The noise ahead grows stronger and drums can be heard.

'Don't like this,' Huva says. A moment later she turns sharply when he taps her shoulder, 'People behind us.'

A large crowd is noisily making their way towards them. Tula acts immediately and runs until there is a bend in the road, out of sight she dives into a clump of thorn bushes.

'Hang on I nearly came unstuck.'

'Shush! Be quiet!' Tula rubs her scratched arm, where her cape is torn, but in spite of the stinging pain she stays still. A group of men appear; they are a ragged lot. They wear an assortment of dusty grey and brown woollen smocks, which are old and worn. Many have leather sandals; not unlike her own.

'They must be soldiers as they carry weapons,' she whispers to Huva.

Some men are singing and swinging their long-bows as they march. The words are unfamiliar to her but it is a cheerful tune. Others hang their heads and do not sing. There are mutterings as the men wipe their brown-streaked faces, patches of sweat show on their tunics. A few silently lag behind, their feet are heavy. Carts drawn by oxen follow; two are loaded with barrels, another with long-bows. There is a thunder of hooves as three riders gallop past. The riders are better dressed and carry swords by their sides. They must be in charge, Tula thinks.

'We wait until they are gone.' Huva whispers.

Tula nods and only moves forward after the group disappears around another bend. Now she keeps a wary eye out for any movement behind her. She leaves a long distance between herself and the dust cloud created by the marching soldiers.

'Look the sea is over there, where the many buildings are! We could smell it, if it wasn't for the smoke and stink of gun powder. There's a war going on here.' Tula's mouth droops at the corners, 'We could've picked a better time to visit.'

'Shall we turn back?'

Tula shakes her head, but alarm shows in her eyes.

As they get closer she sees the water packed with war ships and men running to and fro on the decks. It is a chaotic scene. There seems to be cannon everywhere, their booms fill the air. On the shore there is a walled town, outside of which soldiers mill around the tents. Some men sit on the grass, chewing on lumps of hard cheese and stale pieces of bread. Others drink from pouches, which are tied to their waists.

'What's going on? Do you know what happened in 1545? I only know we are in Tudor times.'

'No, never been before. Didn't want to come here, but you made me. Only the bravest of trolls go back in time,' Huva answers in a low growl.

Tula is not surprised to feel a nip on her arm, I wish he'd stop that every time he's unhappy, she thinks.

Some of the soldiers stand in groups; they wear helmets and heavy armour. 'It looks like their jackets have been knitted in metal.' Tula whispers over her shoulder, 'And they have boots, they are better dressed than the lot we saw on the road.'

The area outside the town gate is full; amongst the people some dodgy characters sneak about. A man leers at her, so Tula makes a dash into the middle of the crowd. She holds her breath, Doesn't anyone here ever wash? she thinks.

Everyone is speaking excitedly and gesticulating. One man points to the sea and repeats, 'The French, the French are coming. We are doomed!'

'Jeeps! What's going on?' her words are followed by loud gun fire. Tula crouches down and covers her ears.

'I don't like loud noise,' Huva whimpers and his shadow shakes.

'Get used to it. Look over there at the square building by the shore. Could that be Southsea Castle? Let's go for it!'

Tula is carried along by the crowd to where many colourful tents are raised. People are talking to each other or walking between the tents. She stops and gapes, 'Huva, look at their clothes. Amazing!'

'Yeah, they are the rich people.'

'The velvet gowns must be warm in the sunshine. Look Huva, their dresses are decorated with pearls and beads in all colours. So pretty!'

Huva snorts behind her back, 'The men have trousers ending at the knee, like you.'

'Yes, I dressed to look like a boy.'

Tula stares at a group of ladies; their richly decorated gowns, with full flowing skirts, are made of silk and brocade. Still more beads covers the sides of the hoods, which frame their faces.

'The men have hats with feathers in them. Walk closer, Tula!'

'Why?'

'I want to look.'

Tula moves up to a man; his jacket has beads sewn onto it and a lace collar, on his head a flat hat with a big feather. A sour smell surrounds him and Tula's nose twitches, even the rich people stink, she thinks. Huva's shadow leans over and pulls out the feather, without the man noticing.

Tula moves away quickly. The feather floats through the air, and she sneezes as her nose is tickled with it.

'You're mad,' she hisses. 'We must give it back.' Huva snorts his piggy laugh. The feather blows around in front of her face. 'We'll get into trouble.'

'I want to keep it,' Huva says, 'it's fun.'

Tula has now got the feather in her hand and people are watching her. The expressions on their faces are stern, and one woman points at her. Tula runs back to the man and bows deeply in front of him, 'Yours, Sir, it blew off.' The man's eyebrows shoot up, and he feels his hat for the missing feather. He accepts it with a curt nod.

Not far away is the grey stone castle. By the parapet, along the edge of the roof, a small group stare out to sea. One man in particular stands out from the rest, he commands respect. The people around give him their full attention. He wears a wide robe trimmed with ermine fur, underneath it a linen shirt, which reaches his knees. The jewels sewn onto the shirt, and the rubies on the brim of his hat, glint in the sunlight.

The man next to Tula nudges the woman beside him, 'Look at the castle, the king is there,' he points.

Tula stares with open mouth, 'I don't believe it,' she whispers. 'Pinch me, Huva, so I know I'm not dreaming. That's Henry VIII. I've actually seen him for real. Jeeps!'

'I only pinch when I'm upset, and I'm not. I'm excited because I'm getting the key back,' he whispers in reply.

The tension in the crowd grows and Tula stands on her toes straining to see, 'Something is going on. I need a place where I can see properly.'

'The key first.'

'In a minute, must see this!'

'No, now!' Huva pinches her arm.

'Later,' Tula hisses, 'and stop it!'

She makes for a small mound behind her, where people have gathered for a view of the battle that is taking place at sea. Tula reaches the top and manages to squeeze her way to the front.

'Jeeps, this is wicked!' she calls out. Ships are facing each other; some carry the French flag. Cannon are firing from both directions and the decks are lined with archers, their arrows fill the air. Four much larger ships each with four sails dominate the others. They are impressive and are flying the English white flag with the red cross. Green and white streamers of the Tudor colours are attached to each mast and proudly flutter in the wind. Tula takes in the sight of these heavy timber ships, where large cannon poke out from the gun ports on the sides. She jumps up and down and bumps into a woman next to her.

'Wow! This will make a super exciting essay.'

The woman, who wears a simple woollen grey dress, stares suspiciously at Tula from underneath her white linen cap and moves away.

Huva's shadow shifts on her back, 'Careful, people are watching you.' The whisper can barely be heard.

Now what's happening? Her attention is drawn back to the battle. The people gesticulate and point out to sea. One of the big ships turns sideways in an awkward movement and tilts. 'There is something wrong,' Tula holds her breath. The archers raise their long bows but are unsteady on their feet. They slide about on deck unable to shoot off their arrows. The ship leans heavily. The crowd have grown silent, unable to believe what they are seeing.

At last a man speaks up, his face is white, 'Mary Rose is floundering. May the Lord help us.'

'Nay, it can't be. She won't sink.' A woman pulls at his sleeve.

Tula strains her neck, 'Jeeps, the Mary Rose!' Her mouth falls open and she goes weak at the knees. She is too excited not to share this with

Huva, so she whispers over her shoulder, 'We've read about her at school.'

The woman keeps on repeating, 'The Mary Rose can't sink.'

'Will it?' A whisper.

'It will,' Tula mutters, but only loud enough for Huva to hear.

A moment later people on the shore are running about, they shout and point to the Mary Rose. There are pitiful calls for help from the men in the water and small boats are launched to save them. Cannon are still firing from the other ships and the noise is deafening.

'The key!' Huva pinches her shoulder. 'Come on! Don't want to spend time here.' He pinches her again.

'One more minute, I want to see this!' Her words are followed by another pinch, harder this time.

'Ouch! Don't do that. All right, all right! We'll go and find it. Those poor soldiers! Better not watch this anyway.' Tula turns her head away from the sea and the sinking ship.

Urged on by Huva, she makes her way towards the castle and the hidden key. Different languages are spoken around them; one of them she knows is Spanish. I can pretend I'm a foreigner, as I speak differently to these people, she thinks.

Closer to the castle Tula can see that the high walls are surrounded by a waterless moat. The only way in is over a footbridge guarded by a soldier.

'This isn't a castle. It's a fortress!' Tula

exclaims.

'Shush! The soldier is watching you!'

About five metres from the bridge Huva whispers again, 'I'll search the castle as a shadow. I must find the key on my own, that's the rule. Wait here.' He slips away.

Tula is startled as the soldier walks up to her, 'Move on,' he grunts.

She moves back, but is forced to move further away still, as he pokes her stomach with his musket. She sits down on the grass and waits for Huva's return. All around her people talk excitedly; there is much dismay over the sinking of the Mary Rose. The soldier is suspicious of me, she thinks, as he stretches out his long neck and glares in her direction. Where is Huva? He is taking ages.

'I'm back.' A whisper in her ear.

'Good. Have you got the key?'

'Yes and no.'

'Come on! Have you got it or not?'

'Found it, it was easy. The key is made of troll gold and I can smell it out. It was in the wall in front of the king. As I loosened the stone, the key fell onto the floor. One of his men picked it up and gave it to him.'

'Oh no!'

'Afraid so. We've got to get it.'

'How?'

'You'll stop him when he walks past, I'll pinch it back.'

'No way. You're mad!'

'Quick. Here he comes!'

'I won't do it!' Tula mutters.

People near them bow deeply. She hears murmurings of, 'Your Majesty,' as he passes by.

Tula bows deeply too, but lifts her head to catch a glimpse of the king as he approaches. His cheeks are bright red and clash with his ginger moustache and beard.

'He is very angry,' Huva whispers.

'That doesn't surprise me. He has just lost his favourite ship and many men.'

'He is fat.'

'Yes, no wonder he is limping carrying all that weight.'

'Do it now!' Huva pokes her back.

'Do what?'

'Talk to him! Hurry! Soon too late.'

'No way! I won't.'

But Huva gives her a push, so hard that she stumbles out in front of the king, 'Your Majesty', she croaks, 'a word, please.'

The king halts but only for a moment, he dismisses her with a wave of his hand, his small eyes sweep past her. To her horror the king stumbles and would have fallen heavily, but one of his aides comes to his help. Oh, no! Huva did that, she thinks.

But it is only Tula who knows, as Huva cannot be seen. She bends down to pick up the king's hat, which has fallen off, but strong arms grip her and she is dragged away from the king. 'Are you mad, boy? To charge the king is treason.'

The soldier from the bridge runs up to them, 'I saw him waiting here to attack the king. It's him all right.'

Everyone stares at Tula, who listens astonished. The king's guard loosen his grip for a moment and she does not hesitate. She tears herself free and takes off as a frightened rabbit. The chase is on. People run after her. 'Stop traitor, stop traitor!'

'Got you!' A man jerks her to a halt, by grabbing the collar of her cape. Swiftly she releases the clasp, which holds it, and runs on. She also realizes that Huva is not with her. From the corner of her eye she sees a young man lunge forward, and he brings her down with a flying tackle. The other man has caught up with them and pulls her up roughly. 'What have you got to say for yourself?' He shakes her, 'Speak up! Confess your crime!' Tula's mouth is dry; she is unable to utter a single word.

'Had your tongue cut out? A mute are you? You'll be in front of a judge in the morning. It's hanging for you.' His grip on her arm hurts her.

The blood rushes to her head, she stutters and tries to protest, but fright has robbed her of her voice. Her legs buckle beneath her, everything goes dark, and she falls to the ground.

GUNVOR JOHANSSON

Tula opens her eyes and takes in the scene around her, but quickly shuts them again. 'Oh no, not this', she moans inwardly and forces herself to look again. She is on a patch of grass, leaning against the mud wall, which surrounds the town. It is not far from the soldiers' tents. Like the rough people next to her, she is bound hand and foot. A wooden cart is parked nearby. We are prisoners, she thinks. That smelly man next to me is scratching all the time, he must be our jailer. Bet he's got fleas. The stench is everywhere; she tries not to breathe too deeply.

Some men are sitting up, all look exhausted. Others are lying down to sleep, their faces rest on the mud. Dirt and sweat patches cling to their ragged tunics.

An old woman puts down a wooden bowl and tankard by the side of the jailer, who is slumped against the wall. A few coins are exchanged. I haven't even got any money to buy food, Tula thinks. Inside the bowl; she can see lumps of gristle floating in a grey fatty liquid. She pulls back sharply, Yuk! It smells of wet wool. It makes her retch. The jailer takes a swig from the tankard, he slurps loudly, and wipes his mouth with the back of his hand. The tankard is also wooden and none too clean. If only I could have a drink too, she licks her dry lips. But if I drink or eat anything here, it's bound to make me ill. Everything is so dirty. The thought of food makes her tummy rumble.

The man glares at her, his thick lips pursing. He pulls the revolting stew closer to him, 'You can look, but you ain't having none of this. You won't need food where you're going.' He nods towards the wooden cart, 'You'll be gone soon and good riddance! If it were me, I'd leave you scabby lot to the French. They could be here anytime now that the Mary Rose is gone.'

Tula ignores his ramblings; I know the French aren't coming, she thinks. They'll soon turn round and go home, but I'm in big trouble here. If I escape hanging, drinking the water will kill me. Only Huva can save me, and he must hurry! But where is he?

GUNVOR JOHANSSON

Tula looks at the cart and squeezes her eyes shut, she cannot bear the sight of it, 'Please, please let Huva find me!'

The next second she sits bolt upright. There is a whisper in her ear, 'I'll help you. But first I'll work my magic spell to make the others sleep. Be ready!'

Tula nods.

A light shadow moves in front of the prisoners, it is unnoticeable unless you look for it. One by one the men drop off to sleep, the jailer last of all.

'I'll untie your hands.' A whisper.

'Did you get the key?'

'Yes, when the king fell, I pinched it back from the folds of his robe. Keep it safe for me.' A key appears in front of her.

Tula puts it in her pocket and sighs with relief as the rope around her ankles loosens.

The prisoner on her right is stirring; his eyes blink open. The spell has not worked on him. When he sees that Tula is untied, he smirks at her, 'Free me, or I'll call out.' He is a tall man with a thin narrow face and cold eyes.

'I haven't got time,' Tula protests getting onto her knees.

'You'll have even less, boy, if you don't. Now do it!'

She tugs at the rope around the man's legs, 'It's no good. The knot's too hard.'

The other prisoners are restless, several are yawning. Tears roll down her cheeks, 'Jeeps, they are waking up already,' sweat breaks out on her forehead.

'Please, please help,' she whispers through

gritted teeth, and at once the knot becomes soft in her hand and easily undone. 'Thank you, Huva,' her lips barely move. She crawls to the man's back and releases his hands.

The next second he grasps her arm in an iron grip and her face is pressed up against his chest. The dankness of his smock gets into her nose, 'Now you're coming with me. You're a handy little thief to have around.' The prisoner pulls her up roughly and drags her away from the stirring group, forcing her along.

'Let me go! Let me go!' Tula digs in her heels, but amongst the chaos and black smoke of the gunfire no one takes any notice.

Except for the jailer. He is awake and points in their direction. He runs after them but without warning he falls flat on his face. Well done, Huva, she thinks.

The prisoner sprints to hide behind one of the tents and drags her with him. He takes a rope from his pocket, 'With this round your wrist, boy, there'll be no running away. You'll go where I go.'

'Huva, where are you?' Tula cries out and

kicks the prisoner's leg.

'Who's that you're calling?' The man shifts his head from side to side, his eyes narrowing.

All at once Huva's weight is on her back; he has jumped up and stands with one foot on each of her shoulders.

He is a troll, not a shadow anymore.

He is the same height as the prisoner and stares him in the face, 'Boo!' he shouts. A deep growl starts to grow from inside his chest, and it gains in strength, until it explodes in a deafening roar. The colour drains from the prisoner's face and his eyes bulge, with a loud scream he lets go of the rope and runs for his life.

'That was amazing. He was terrified. Wish I'd seen your face, Huva, you must've been very frightening.' And she knows in that instant that something has happened to Huva; he has changed. 'The Troll Court won't think you're a coward anymore, you're a proper scary troll now.'

Huva is a shadow again and chuckles loudly behind her. People scurry to and fro, horses gallop past. Cannon fire and drums fills the air. Tula starts to run, she is in a hurry to leave what has happened behind her, and makes for the road out of town.

After a while she sits down exhausted on the grass verge, 'I want to go home.'

'We will! We'll climb the ladder and on the last rung, we'll be whisked back.' Tula listens in wonder to his calm and strong voice and she is no longer scared.

Again she sets off at speed, but it is too warm and she slows down. There is a lot of activity on the road. Soldiers are making their way to the battle and towns' people are moving away from it.

A cart draws up beside her, 'Jump in boy, save your legs.' The man's voice is husky.

'No!' a voice from behind her.

Tula shakes her head and slows down to keep her distance. The man mutters and holds up his fist. The cart moves on.

'You did right. Nasty man,' Huva whispers. 'Don't worry, Tula, we'll soon be at the barn.'

'There it is!' Tula cries out as they reach a

bend in the road.

'Hang on, I'm falling off.' Huva clings on as she runs.

At the barn she grabs the wooden handle and the smell of dusty straw greets her as she flings the door open, but that is not all. Inside the barn two hard-looking men stare back at her. One is short and stocky, with angry eyes and a bald head. The other is tall and lean and a black beard frames his red, pock-marked face. Several muskets lie in a pile on the floor. 'Oops!' Tula takes a deep breath and turns on her heel.

Too late!

'Ughh!' she cries, as she is grabbed by the man with the beard and pulled backwards into the barn. Tula fights to get away, she beats her fists on his leather jerkin, which reeks of sweat.

'Not so fast. You've seen too much. You're going nowhere.' But he lets go when she kicks his leg.

'Nay, you shouldn't have done that,' grunts the bald man and moves towards her with a snarl on his lips. All at once he stumbles on an invisible object, and hits the floor with a bang.

Good job, Huva, she thinks, she knows that he is no longer on her back. The man struggles to get up, and crawls towards her. The bearded man has stopped rubbing his leg. His small black eyes bore into her and he lunges forward.

'Oh, my goodness! He's mad!' Tula shrinks back, and looks wildly around her for an escape.

'The ladder!' A voice in her ear.

She leaps onto the ladder, aware that Huva's shadow is in front of her. Half way up, she sees a hand claw at her trousers and dirty finger nails pull at her sandal. She kicks out and the sandal falls off, but now the man climbs after her.

At that moment, from above her, comes Huva's blood curling roar, which grows stronger by the second. The man falls to the floor screaming and crawls towards the door. His companion pulls him up and together they stumble out of the barn. Over their shoulders they stare back, their faces are white and terror shows in their eyes.

Tula tightens her grip on the ladder, Huva has come out of his shadow and he scares her too. His chest is blown up and his eyes flash with fire. His lips are curled back and orange flames leap from his black hair. 'You're burning,' she screams.

At her scream Huva becomes a normal troll, 'No, it's not for real, it's an illusion. Troll magic, I couldn't do it before. Now I can, thanks to you.' His face glows with pride.

'Why thanks to me?'

'It works; to protect you.'

'Wow! That was incredibly scary, Huva. Your voice is not whiny anymore, and you've saved me again.'

Huva turns bright red and he scurries onto

the last rung, where he disappears in a white cloud. Tula hurries after him, and in a moment she is back on the Century Ladder by his side. The climb up to the Leaning Stone begins.

Once inside the Leaning Stone Tula points at the door marked Troll Land, 'We've made it! You're free to go home. You'd better hurry.' She fumbles in her pocket and holds out his key, 'Here it is. You've saved my life twice.' Her smile is replaced by a frown and she adds, 'I've finally got rid of you.'

'If you got used to me, could you like me a bit?' Huva's large black eyes stare up at her unblinking.

'Yes, perhaps....' Tula looks at his rosy face and shakes her head, 'That's not going to happen. Please, ask Sten to let me out.'

'I heard that!' A gravelly voice fills the room followed by a loud rumble. Daylight appears as Sten opens his mouth to allow her out.

Huva follows.

Moss flaps open to reveal Sten's eyes, 'Well done you two. I hear that Huva has passed the test and is now a proper troll. Welcome home, Huva, and it's been nice to meet you, Tula.'

'Thank you, Sten. You too!'

Tula turns to Huva, 'Your people are waiting in Troll Land. You'd better go now.'

'Suppose,' he answers with a mischievous smile. He does not meet her eyes, 'I will…soon,' he adds with a smirk on his lips.

Tula walks away, but turns to wave to Huva, who waves back. He looks lonely on his own in front of that huge stone. I hope he'll be happy

in Troll Land, but I'm pleased to be
rid of him. At least I think
so. She shakes off the
thoughts and takes
the forest path,
which leads to her
home. She limps as
she is only wearing
one sandal, the other one is in a barn
hundreds of years away.

Already she thinks of the amazing essay, she
will write about Henry VIII and the sinking of the
Mary Rose. How impressed her teacher will be
when she reads it! Tula does not turn around;
so does not notice the shadow which follows
her from tree to tree.

THE END

**Look out for the next book
in the series**

Turn the page and read the first chapter now.

GUNVOR JOHANSSON

GUNVOR JOHANSSON

Tula kneels down by the side of the forest lake and in the clear water she can see her own reflection. The water has a green tinge and when she splashes her cheeks with it, it feels very cold.

'Oh,' she cries out. By the side of her face another one has appeared. The eyes are huge and a mass of wiry hair covers the head, from which pointed ears stick out. It is Huva the troll.

'Oh no, not you again!' she moans. 'Why don't you go home? I won't come down the Century Ladder with you again. One trip back in time is enough for me.'

There is a scurry and at the next moment Huva shins up the trunk of a tall fir tree. The small figure crawls out onto a large branch, which overhangs the lake.

'Don't try it on again,' she pleads. 'I won't save you. Don't jump, Huva!'

'Trolls can't swim.' Huva calls back.

'Well, then you'll drown.' Tula glares up into the branches, hands on her hips.

'You wouldn't let me!'

'Just watch me!' Tula limps as she walks away. On one foot, she is wearing only a wet sock. 'Ouch!' She bends down to remove a pine needle, which was stuck in the wool.

Behind her, she can see Huva crawl back towards the tree-trunk. She smiles, she knew that would work. Trolls are scared of water, they never wash. Huva had told her this when they first met a few days ago. Before that she had not known that trolls live in this forest. 'They should only live in Fairy Tales and certainly not here in Scotland,' she sighs.

Tula spins around, because in the next

second she hears a loud splash. She sprints back in time to see Huva's black spiky hair disappear beneath the surface. His yellow waist-coat is curled around his shoulders and floats above him. His head comes up; he has swallowed water and he spits and splutters. Tula wades out and as he disappears for a second time, she grabs hold of the waist-coat and pulls, 'Got you!'

Huva's head appears above the water line, he is gasping for breath. Tula drags him ashore; she grabs him by his feet and stands him on his head.

She wriggles him about, 'That should get the water out of you. God job you're only little and not heavy.'

Huva coughs so hard it makes him gulp for air, 'Let go of me,' he squeaks, when finally he is able to speak.

Tula lowers him down, 'OK, you're safe. You know what this means, now that I have saved your life again. Bother!'

'Yes,' Huva squeals, his voice is not yet back to normal. 'Have to be your obedient servant once more. Don't be cross. Fell in, it was an accident.'

Tula sets her lips in a tight line and her eyes are narrowing. She stares at Huva; he is so small, he barely reaches to her waist. His waist-coat and red shorts cling to his hairy body. The water drips off his bushy eyebrows and large pointed ears. Her anger gone, she tries hard not to smile.

'You want rid of me, Tula. Why don't you like me?' Huva hangs his head.

'How can I, when you're not supposed to exist? You are a troll! Every time I look at you, I have to pinch myself. Are you sure you're real?'

'You know I am. Today I took you back in time, down the Century Ladder. We can go again, to a different century. We should, we should, we should!' Huva jumps up and down.

'Calm down!' Tula puts a hand on his shoulders to still him. 'Yes, it was amazing! But it's too dangerous. Why don't you go back to Troll Land and leave me alone?'

'Must stay with you.'

'I know! You'll have to save my life first, because I saved yours just now. The stupid law

4

of your land says so,' Tula says glumly. 'We're back where we started. Well, you've saved me once before. Guess you could again, and I'll finally be free of you.'

Huva nods his head vigorously, smiling now.

'But it's a bother!' Tula frowns, 'At least you don't smell so much, now that you've been in the lake. Come on then. I must go home. Mum will be frantic, I've been away for ages.'

'No you haven't, Tula. Down the Century Ladder time hardly moves at all.'

'What do you mean?'

'It's nearly the same time as when we left this morning. You've only been away for a few minutes.'

'I don't believe you!' Tula holds up her wrist, 'Oh, I forgot. I left my watch and mobile at home.' The watch had been her tenth birthday present from her parents, only a few weeks ago, and she had not taken it off until now. 'They didn't have watches in the sixteenth century, where we've just been.' Tula pulls at the wet sock on her right foot, 'But I left something behind, hundreds of years back in time. My other sandal is still in that barn.'

Huva's big nose twitches, 'Come on! Let's have another adventure. You did like the excitement.'

'Yes, I did! And if what you say is true...' Tula stares into the distance with a dreamy expression on her face. A moment later she laughs out loud and claps her hands, 'Terrific! We can go back in time to anywhere we like and have lots of adventures! Nobody would know we've gone, or miss us!'

'That's right,' Huva smiles at her mischievously. 'So will you come with me down the ladder again?'

'Might do.'

'I am a proper troll now, thanks to you. Not afraid of anything. I can scare anybody. Look at me!' Huva beats his chest and yellow flames leap out of his hair, his eyes flash. A deep growl builds up in his chest.

Tula waves her hands, 'OK, stop it! I know you can do it.'

'I learnt it when you were in danger, to save your life.'

Tula nods, 'That's true.' She takes a deep breath, 'You're right. It was terribly exciting! I will come down the ladder, just once more…' After a few moments she shakes her head, 'No, Huva, I won't do it. Today we only just made it back alive. Sorry!'

But Huva is not listening to her. His ears are pricked up, he stands very still and stares into the trees. Tula is aware that the forest has gone quiet, the birds have stopped singing. Nothing in these woods frightens her; she knows them well, she has lived here all her life. Her dad, the Forest Ranger, has often taken her with him to explore. Now all at once there is a strange silence …

Made in the USA
Charleston, SC
11 November 2016